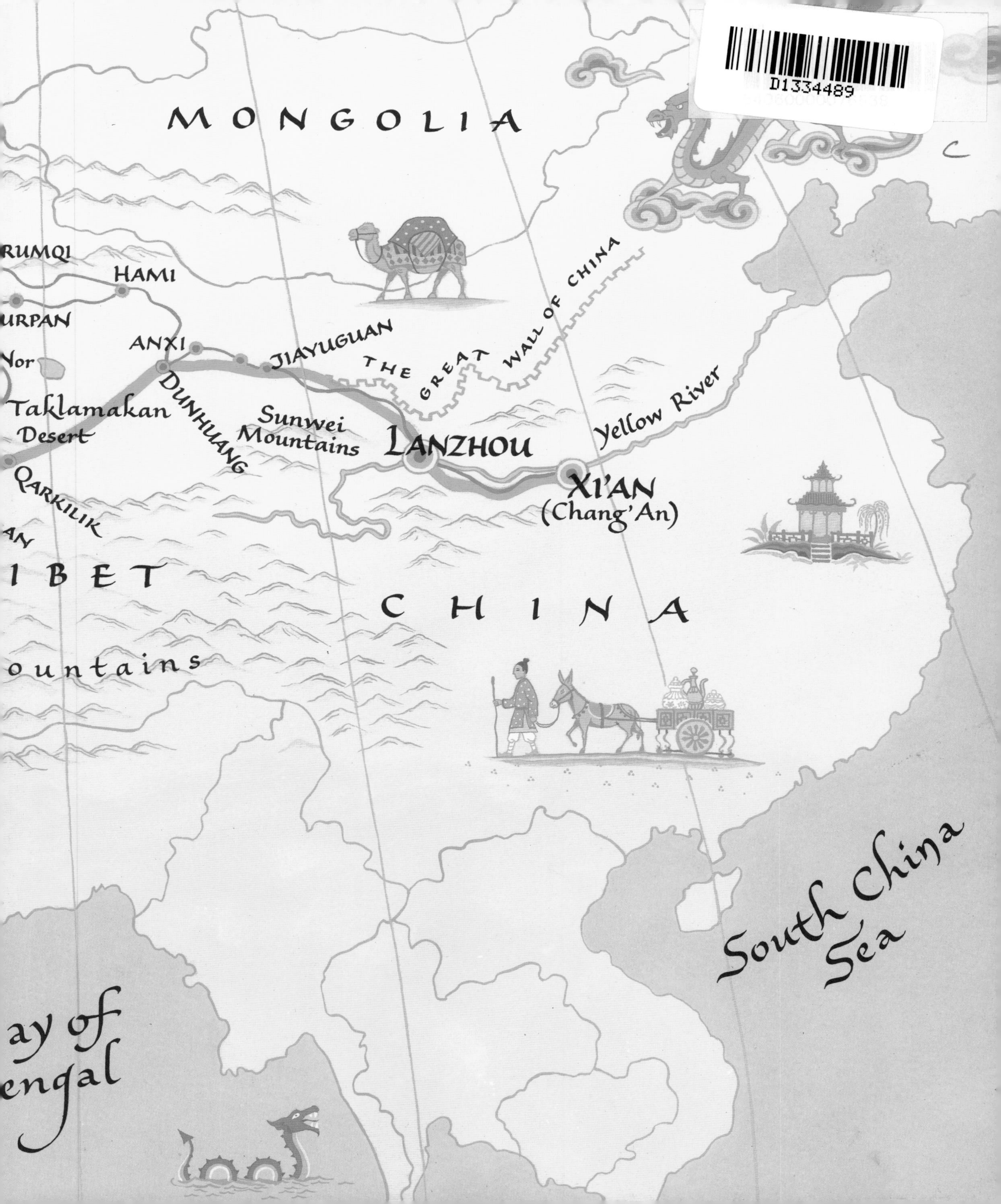
MONGOLIA
RUMQI
HAMI
URPAN
ANXI
Nor
JIAYUGUAN
THE GREAT WALL OF CHINA
DUNHUANG
Taklamakan Desert
Sunwei Mountains
LANZHOU
Yellow River
XI'AN
(Chang'An)
QARKILIK
AN
IBET
CHINA
ountains
South China Sea
ay of
engal

Stories from The Silk Road

For Jagdish — N. M.

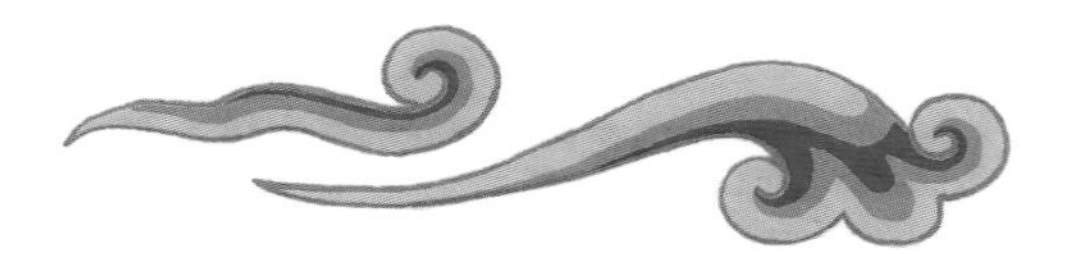

Barefoot Collections
an imprint of
Barefoot Books
PO Box 95
Kingswood
Bristol
BS30 5BH

This book has been printed on 100% acid-free paper
Illustrations were prepared in gouache on 140lb watercolour paper

Graphic design by Jennie Hoare, Bradford on Avon
Typeset in Minion 13pt
Colour separation by Unifoto, Cape Town
Printed and bound in Hong Kong by South China Printing Co. (1988) Ltd

ISBN 1 901223 21 3

British Library Cataloguing-in-Publication Data:
a catalogue record for this book is available from the British Library

1 3 5 7 9 8 6 4 2

Acknowledgements
My grateful thanks to Professor Roderick Whitfield of the School of Oriental and African Studies, University of London, noted scholar on Dunhuang and the Silk Road, for his invaluable help in suggesting corrections to the text. Also to the peoples of today's Silk Road for their welcome and for the unforgettable glimpse into their lives and heritage. And to my family, for putting up with my absences during my trips along the Silk Road. — C. G.

Stories from The Silk Road

retold by
Cherry Gilchrist

illustrated by
Nilesh Mistry

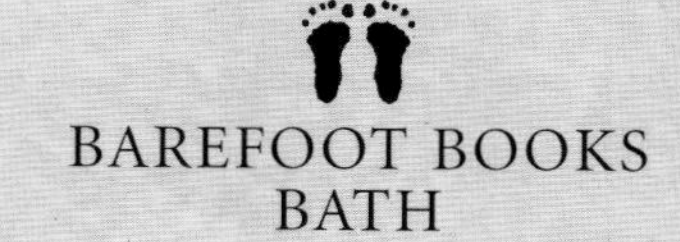

BAREFOOT BOOKS
BATH

Contents

Contents

INTRODUCTION

THE SILK ROAD IS THE OLD TRADE ROUTE BETWEEN EAST AND WEST. It began at the old Chinese capital of Chang'an, now called Xian, and carried on right into Central Asia. It is hard to say exactly where it ended — the main stretch led to cities like Samarkand and Khiva, but some caravans followed the Silk Road to Syria, Turkey, Jordan, and even into Western Europe. There were also many choices of route along the way; one much-used turning led south into India, for instance. The Silk Road was really a network of branching roads, but travellers all used it for the same purpose — to take desirable goods between East and West.

No one knows quite when this trading began, but people probably started to use some parts of the route from about 2000 BC or earlier, trading jade, minerals and other precious stones. By about 200 BC it was a proper trade route, and so it remained until the fourteenth century, when it was mainly replaced by safer and more convenient sea routes from Asia to Europe.

We call it the Silk Road because silk was indeed one of the most important goods traded between China and the West. But many other items were carried along it too, from the West to the East as well, such as glass, carpets, incense, jade, and even exotic kinds of fruit and vegetables. Over the years people acquired an appetite for novel foreign imports, and were often prepared to pay huge sums of money for them. Gradually, of course, the unusual precious things became more common. Nowadays we do not think twice about chopping up a cucumber or buying a cotton shirt, but both of these items were once expensive rarities when they were traded along the Silk Road.

The Silk Road was also an important route for the exchange of ideas. Knowledge of astronomy, medicine and science passed along it, and religions were spread via it, such as Buddhism, Islam and the ancient Persian religion of Zoroastrianism. Art too changed and developed because of this exchange, so that in the far reaches of western China today you can see Buddhist paintings which were influenced by European and, above all, Indian art.

Many empires rose and fell in the territories crossed by the Silk Road. The Sogdian, Kushan and Parthian empires have long since passed away, as well as many kingdoms, such as Kashgaria and Gandhara. The peoples of the Silk Road have also moved around, often displaced by invaders, especially by the Mongol hordes who conquered huge areas of Asia, Central Asia and Europe in the thirteenth century.

However, the Mongols did bring a kind of peace to the Silk Road. Previously it had been almost impossible for travellers to go from one end to the other without interruption. Although some early travellers did manage to reach their final destinations along the Silk Road, this was not a reliable way to trade or travel. Somewhere along the way there were always wars, rebellions and kings who did not allow foreigners in. So the normal practice was for a caravan to set off, often with a train of several hundred beasts, until it reached a particular staging point along the way. Here the caravan drivers would hand their goods over to the next team of camel men or muleteers, and perhaps load up their own beasts with some goods coming in the opposite direction before heading for home. Only in later years, from the thirteenth century onwards, was it in general safe and practical for a caravan and its men, or even independent travellers, to complete the whole journey themselves.

You can still travel the Silk Road today, and see many of the old cities, monasteries and staging posts that guided travellers on their journey. You can see many of the peoples of the Silk Road too — Uighurs, Kirghiz and Tajiks, for instance — and their traditional way of life. You can visit busy livestock markets and wander in bazaars where raisins, knives, silk and beaten copper are traded, where neighbouring peoples still haggle fiercely over special goods that they cannot get at home. But for our journey now, we will step backwards in time and travel the Silk Road during the years of its real glory.

CHERRY GILCHRIST

Woven Wind

Hello! Do you want to come with me down the Silk Road? We'll start our journey at Chang'an, the old capital of China. Then we'll travel westwards, through deserts and up icy mountains, until at last we come to the splendid city of Samarkand. You're lucky that you're with me. You won't have to trudge alongside a camel for months, getting thirsty and hungry, and fighting off robbers. I'm the Spirit of the Silk Road and I'll whisk you along on my silken threads, faster than a flying dragon, lighter than a bird. They call silk 'woven wind', and you'll soon see why!

Are you ready to set off? I'll tell you more about silk as we go. Do you see those trees over there? Those are mulberry trees, and their leaves are the only kind of food that silkworms can eat. Those women picking the leaves have to feed the silkworms every half an hour. After a month each worm will be ten thousand times heavier than it was! Then it will spin itself a cocoon of silk thread, getting ready to turn itself into a moth. But before that can happen, each cocoon is dropped into boiling water and the silk is reeled off, ready for spinning and weaving.

They say silk cloth was first made in China about three thousand years ago. The Chinese guarded the secret of making silk very carefully. The Romans were fighting the Parthians when they first saw silk. The sight of their enemy's bright, silk banners was such a shock that they lost the battle, but soon they came to desire silk more than gold. It was very expensive to buy, and to start with only the most important Romans were allowed to

wear it. That was true in China too: at first only the Emperor and his court wore this beautiful material. Before long, though, in both empires everybody began to dress up in silk.

People in the West tried to guess what silk was. Some thought that it was a kind of down that grew on a special tree. Others thought that it came from the inside of a huge kind of spider-beetle with eight legs. At last, so the story goes, a Chinese princess who was about to marry a foreign prince managed to smuggle some silkworm eggs out of the country in her headdress. She couldn't bear the thought of married life without silk! And so the secret escaped to the West.

As you can see in these villages that we're passing through, making silk is usually women's work. Every farm has its mulberry garden and silk house. These peasant women stay up at night, tending their silkworms and spinning the thread by moonlight.

In China the chief goddess of silk is called Lei Tsu, or sometimes Hsi Ling. She is said to have discovered silk threads one day when she accidentally dropped a silkworm's cocoon into a cup of hot tea!

But here's a story about another goddess of silk. It's called 'The Bride with the Horse's Head'.

THE BRIDE WITH THE HORSE'S HEAD

'OH, WHAT A TERRIBLE THING HAS HAPPENED TO US!'

Ma-t'ou Niang's mother was weeping bitterly. She hid her face in her silken sleeve as her daughter tried to comfort her. 'Why did they take him? What harm had he ever done to them?'

'Oh, Mother, try and calm yourself,' said Ma-t'ou Niang. 'Perhaps they will release my father unharmed.'

But in her heart she was afraid that this would not be so. Her father had been seized by robbers three days ago. A gang armed with cudgels had taken him prisoner while he was walking peacefully through their mulberry orchard.

'I don't know where they came from! I don't know where they took him!' sobbed his wife.

'Well then, Mother,' said Ma-t'ou Niang, 'perhaps we should wait patiently. They will come back with demands for money, or they will let him go when they find out that we are not a rich family.'

But her mother's tears flowed all the faster. 'We have no one in our family to protect us now that my brother is dead, no one to send in search of my dear husband. Oh, if only there was someone! I would gladly give your hand in marriage, Ma-t'ou Niang, to the person who brings back my husband alive!'

Suddenly there was a sound of clattering hooves, and a horse came galloping past them. Her husband's favourite horse had broken out of his stable and was running away. Over the fence he leaped, and was gone.

The two women could hardly believe their eyes. 'So now I have to lose a good horse as well!' exclaimed Ma-t'ou Niang's mother. 'Is there no end to our bad luck?'

'No, Mother — I think he heard us. I think he's gone to rescue Father!' said Ma-t'ou Niang.

'Impossible!' retorted her mother angrily. 'He is only a horse, isn't he? How could he understand?'

The girl held her peace. But she was right. A few days later, early in the morning, they spied the horse trotting proudly homewards. And on his back was her father.

'Hello there! Greetings!' he shouted to his wife and daughter, who had come running out to meet him. 'The horse has brought me back safely. What a fine beast he is!'

When the horse was comfortably stabled again, and Ma-t'ou Niang's father had sat down to eat a hearty breakfast, he told his family what had happened.

'The robbers were keeping me locked up in an old storehouse. They were angry when I couldn't offer them a handsome reward for my freedom. Perhaps they would have killed me. I was in despair, worrying about you both. Then, last night, suddenly I heard a loud noise. It sounded as though

someone was trying to break down the big wooden doors of the barn where I was being kept prisoner. It wasn't a man, though — it was my horse! He broke down the doors with his hooves, to let me escape. So I quickly jumped on his back and he galloped home with me. I bet those men were surprised to find me gone!'

For the next few days everyone was happy — except the horse. He was very angry because Ma-t'ou Niang's mother had forgotten all about her promise. Whenever he passed the girl, he neighed and kicked out furiously.

Her father was beginning to lose his temper. 'What's the matter with you, beast?' he shouted. 'If you hadn't rescued me back there, I would whip you now!'

Then Ma-t'ou Niang's mother remembered her promise. Her hand flew to her mouth in horror. 'Oh, husband, I promised! I gave my word that the person who rescued you could have the hand of our daughter in marriage!'

'What? Are you crazy? He's not a person, he's an animal! I'll stop his nonsense!' In a blind rage he seized an axe and killed the horse that had saved his life.

Ma-t'ou Niang burst into tears, and would not be consoled. The next day her father, ashamed of himself by now, took the skin off the horse and laid it out in the sun to dry.

A day or two later, Ma-t'ou Niang was on her way to tend the silk-worms in the silkworm house.

'Cut plenty of fresh leaves for them!' called her mother anxiously from the doorway.

Ma-t'ou Niang had to pass the spot where the horse's skin lay. But as she approached the skin, it rose into the air and wrapped itself around her. Now it looked as though Ma-t'ou Niang herself had a horse's head!

Then, before her startled mother could do anything, the skin, with Ma-t'ou Niang inside, flew up into the sky and disappeared from sight.

Her father and mother were grief-stricken. Now they had lost their precious daughter, their only child. And they did not know any way of getting her back.

'If only you hadn't been so hasty!' said Ma-t'ou Niang's mother.

'If only you hadn't been so foolish, making a promise like that!' said her father.

Even the silkworms seemed to know that she was gone, and they didn't gorge themselves greedily on the mulberry leaves or spin their cocoons as they should have done. The trees began to shed some of their leaves, and the garden looked sad and neglected.

'Oh, Ma-t'ou Niang!' sighed her mother. 'If only you could send us a sign, just one sign, to let us know that you're all right.'

She wandered towards the place where her daughter had disappeared. And then, to her astonishment, she saw that once again the horse's skin was lying at the foot of the mulberry tree. But where was her daughter? Her eyes searched the tree anxiously.

Up above, hanging from one of the branches, a little silkworm was spinning its cocoon. And a tiny voice came from it — very faint, but definitely Ma-t'ou Niang's voice.

'Don't weep, Mother,' it said. 'You see, I'm spinning myself a silk gown! It will soon be ready.'

Ma-t'ou Niang's mother rushed back to the house to tell her husband. But when they returned to the spot, both the horse's skin and the silkworm had gone.

'You foolish woman!' said her husband crossly, trying to hide his bitter disappointment. 'You dreamed it all!'

Ma-t'ou Niang's mother shook her head and said nothing.

Then her father looked up into the sky, to hide the tears in his eyes. He was a proud man, but in his heart he was very ashamed at what he had done. Suddenly his tears dried as he saw what was up there.

'Is it really…? Look, look!' He pointed upwards.

Descending from a cloud in the sky, dressed in a beautiful, shimmering silken robe and attended by a whole retinue of servants, was their own dear daughter. She was no longer a silkworm but a beautiful young woman once again.

'Here I am, Mother and Father!' Ma-t'ou Niang sang out joyfully. 'I am one of the Jade Emperor's brides now. The Emperor of Heaven has made me his wife! He says that because I have a kind heart and have done my duty to you on earth, he will reward me by giving me a place in Heaven. There's no need to worry about me any more!'

'Oh, Ma-t'ou Niang!' cried her mother. 'We are so happy to know that you are well. But will we ever see you again? And how will our silkworms

survive? They miss you! They have gone off their food and refuse to spin their cocoons. We shall have no silk!'

'Dear Mother,' said Ma-t'ou Niang, 'don't fret. The Jade Emperor has put me in charge of the silkworms too — of silkworms everywhere — and all the workers who toil to feed them and reel the silk, and all the weavers who make it into fine cloth. I am to look after them all!'

'And what about the horse?' asked her father. 'I am really very sorry. I should never have killed him, and I regret it bitterly.'

'Don't worry about him either, Father,' said Ma-t'ou Niang. 'He knows that you had my best interests at heart. The Jade Emperor has allowed him to be my chief horse in Heaven, and he is very happy to carry me around there.'

Then the young bride slowly began to disappear through the clouds again, smiling and waving at her astonished parents.

When her mother visited her silkworm houses again, she found that the worms were greedily eating the leaves or busy spinning themselves splendid cocoons. The silk that year was some of the best they had ever had.

And from that day to this, Ma-t'ou Niang, the goddess of silk, has looked after the silkworms and the silk workers all over China.

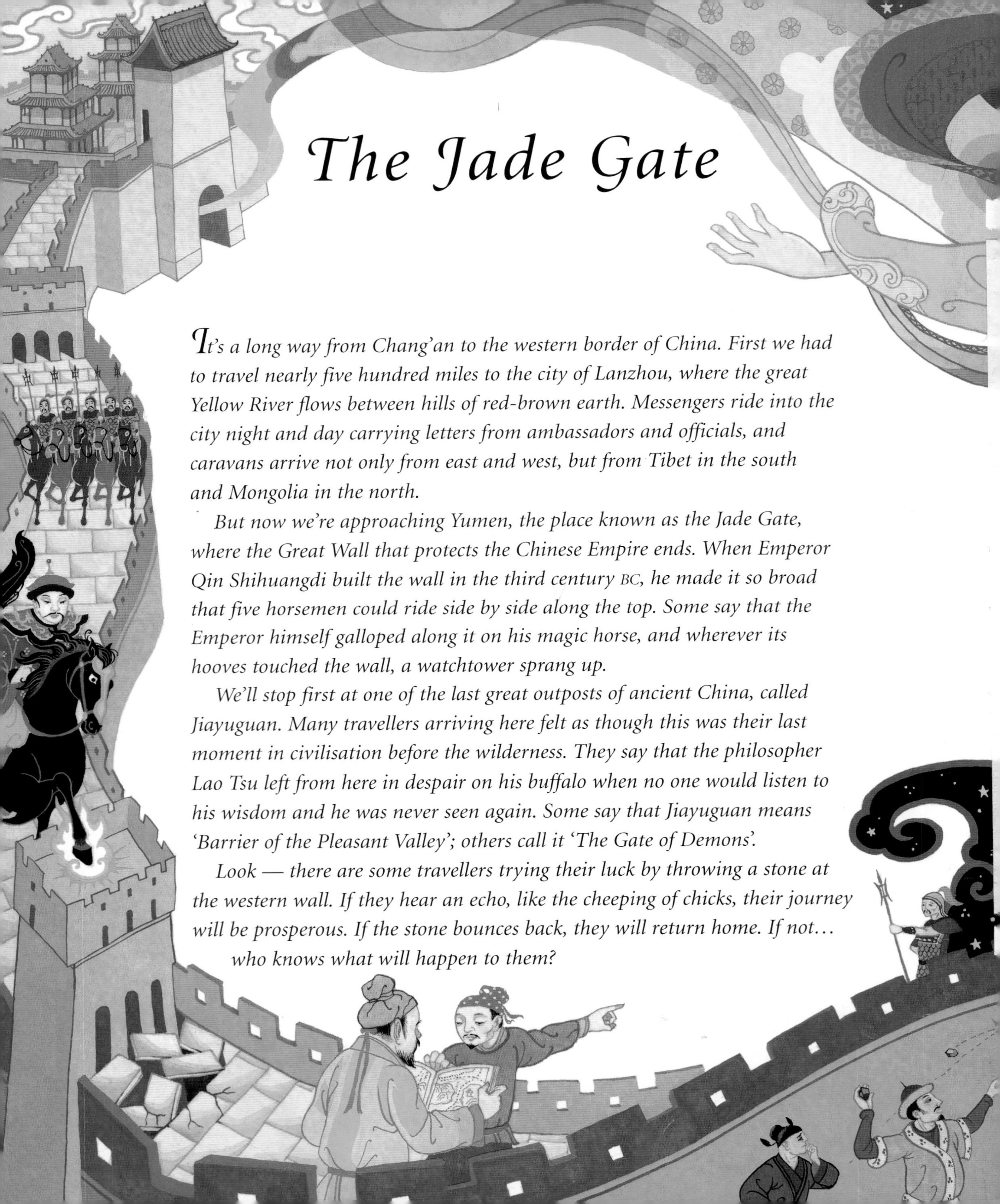

The Jade Gate

It's a long way from Chang'an to the western border of China. First we had to travel nearly five hundred miles to the city of Lanzhou, where the great Yellow River flows between hills of red-brown earth. Messengers ride into the city night and day carrying letters from ambassadors and officials, and caravans arrive not only from east and west, but from Tibet in the south and Mongolia in the north.

But now we're approaching Yumen, the place known as the Jade Gate, where the Great Wall that protects the Chinese Empire ends. When Emperor Qin Shihuangdi built the wall in the third century BC, *he made it so broad that five horsemen could ride side by side along the top. Some say that the Emperor himself galloped along it on his magic horse, and wherever its hooves touched the wall, a watchtower sprang up.*

We'll stop first at one of the last great outposts of ancient China, called Jiayuguan. Many travellers arriving here felt as though this was their last moment in civilisation before the wilderness. They say that the philosopher Lao Tsu left from here in despair on his buffalo when no one would listen to his wisdom and he was never seen again. Some say that Jiayuguan means 'Barrier of the Pleasant Valley'; others call it 'The Gate of Demons'.

Look — there are some travellers trying their luck by throwing a stone at the western wall. If they hear an echo, like the cheeping of chicks, their journey will be prosperous. If the stone bounces back, they will return home. If not… who knows what will happen to them?

But though there are dangers, our Silk Road caravan masters know their routes well. There are even guidebooks which tell them what to take, what to sell and where they will find the best bargains. It took a long time for the traders to acquire this knowledge. In 139 BC, *the Emperor sent a man called Zhang Qian to talk to the tribes in the distant Ferghana Valley. He was captured and kept there for ten years! During this time he married and raised a family. Then, on the way back, he was captured again. He was unlucky as a diplomat, but when he finally got home, he had lots of information about the places he had been to!*

Other travellers along the Silk Road were pilgrims who went to seek Buddhist teachings in India. Buddhism had already come to China, but it was still centred in India, and Chinese Buddhists wanted to make sure that they were following the right teachings. Everyone's favourite pilgrim was a priest called Xuanzang. He had to leave China secretly in AD *629, because foreign travel was forbidden at that time, riding at night to avoid the sentries. He suffered many hardships, but saw many wonders too. When he came back, he wrote a book about his travels, known as* The Record of the Western Regions. *Many stories were told about him, too, in China. The most popular one was called* Journey to the West, *known as* Monkey *in English. In one of the stories in the book, the mischievous monkey god agrees to help the pilgrim Xuanzang on his journey. But travelling with Monkey is never straight-forward — as we shall see.*

MONKEY AND THE RIVER DRAGON

MONKEY IS ONE OF THE MOST MISCHIEVOUS SPIRITS that has ever scampered through Heaven. He is clever, quick, and he can't sit still. He is rude to everyone, even the Jade Emperor, but everyone is fond of him. Monkey could never lead a peaceful life — that would be much too boring!

Now, Monkey has been given a difficult job to do. He has to help a priest travel to the West from China. It's a long and dangerous journey, but the priest, Tripitaka, has promised to find sacred Buddhist writings in India and bring them back to China. He and Monkey are well on their way now, but I'll tell you what happened right at the start of their journey to the West.

Monkey and Tripitaka were freezing cold. They had reached some high mountains and they could hardly climb the steep, icy paths. A terrible wind was blowing around them, and Monkey was beginning to feel very sorry that he'd ever come on this journey at all. He was just thinking that things couldn't get much worse, when of course they did.

'What's that noise?' asked Tripitaka. They could hear the sound of rushing water.

'Oh yes,' said Monkey gloomily. 'I remember now. It's the Eagle Grief River.'

Very soon they came to the edge of the river. Tripitaka was just going to ask why it had such a funny name, when a huge dragon rose up out of the swirling water and came towards them. Tripitaka stared in amazement, but Monkey knew better. He grabbed his master quickly and pushed him up the bank again. Then he ran down to try and save Tripitaka's horse, but he was too late. He got there just in time to see the dragon open its jaws and swallow the poor horse whole.

'Now what am I to do?' asked Tripitaka when Monkey had told him the bad news. 'Oh dear! There's so far to go. And I can't possibly walk.' He felt so sorry for himself that he began to cry.

'Stop that at once!' shouted Monkey angrily. Other people crying made him angry for some reason. Only he was allowed to feel sorry for himself. 'I'll go and find the wretched horse. Maybe I can persuade the dragon to spit him out!'

'Don't be so cross, Monkey,' said a voice from the sky. 'And don't weep, priest. We are divine spirits who've been sent to help you.'

Tripitaka immediately began to bow down reverently.

'Well, which spirits are you?' asked Monkey. 'I know all of you. Just say your names and I'll tick you off the list.'

'Lu Ting and Lu Chia,' said the voice, 'plus the Guardians of the Five Points, the Four Sentinels, and the Eighteen Protectors of Monasteries. The Golden Headed Guardian is always somewhere around too. We take it in turns to look after you.'

'All right — look after the master while I go and sort out that horse,' said Monkey. 'Don't worry about me,' he said to Tripitaka. 'I'll be all right.'

Dear Monkey! First he tightened the belt of his brocade jacket, then he pulled his tiger skin around him, then he took his iron club and shouted down into the depths of the water, 'You useless fish down there! Give me back my horse!'

The dragon was quietly digesting his meal of delicious white horse, and he was furious that someone should disturb him after lunch. He lurched up through the waves and shouted back, 'Who's there? Who dares to make such a noise up there?'

'Give me back my horse!' yelled Monkey again, and swung his club at the dragon's head. The dragon snapped at Monkey with his terrible jaws and slashed at Monkey with his fierce claws. It was a long and dreadful

fight, but Monkey outwitted the dragon every time, until the beast slid back into the river, exhausted. Nothing Monkey could do would bring him out again.

When Monkey told Tripitaka, the priest was not impressed. 'You dealt with a tiger the other day,' he said, 'and you told me that you were good with dragons too. So what's the problem?'

'I'll show you!' shouted Monkey, in a terrible temper again after Tripitaka's insult. 'Just you wait and see who's master!'

He ran back to the river and cast a special spell on the water to stir it up and make it rough. The furious dragon rose up through the waves.

'What kind of a horrible monster are you?' he shouted at Monkey. 'Will I never get rid of you?'

'Just give me back my horse!' Monkey cried impatiently.

'And how can I do that?' asked the dragon. 'It's already inside me, isn't it?'

'I'll beat you with this cudgel!' screamed Monkey. 'Then you'll think of a way to give it back!'

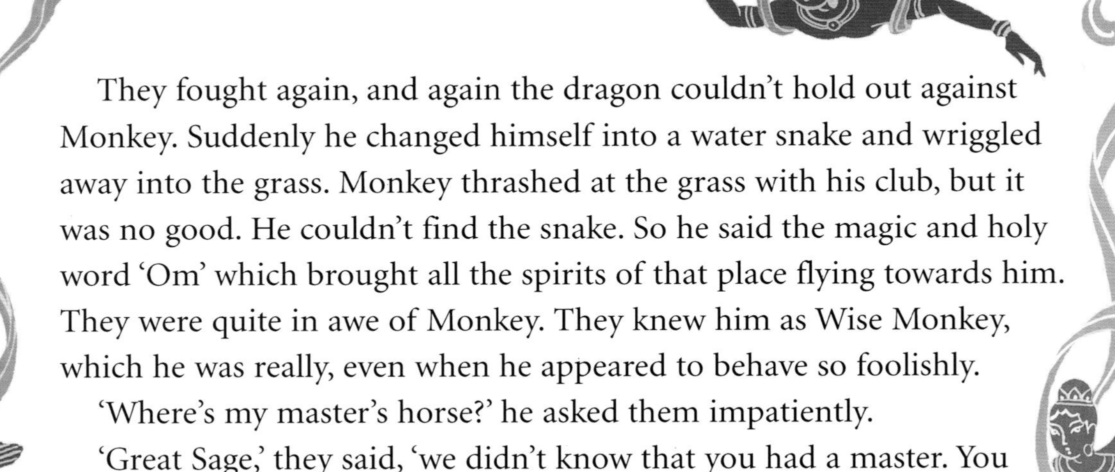

They fought again, and again the dragon couldn't hold out against Monkey. Suddenly he changed himself into a water snake and wriggled away into the grass. Monkey thrashed at the grass with his club, but it was no good. He couldn't find the snake. So he said the magic and holy word 'Om' which brought all the spirits of that place flying towards him. They were quite in awe of Monkey. They knew him as Wise Monkey, which he was really, even when he appeared to behave so foolishly.

'Where's my master's horse?' he asked them impatiently.

'Great Sage,' they said, 'we didn't know that you had a master. You never used to obey anyone, in Heaven or on earth.'

'That was before I got into real trouble with the Jade Emperor and they shut me up in a mountain for five hundred years,' said Monkey. 'They only let me out to do this job. I've got to help this priest, who's going to India to search out Buddhist scriptures. It's a sacred task, you see, and I have to serve him on the journey. So tell me about this dragon.'

'Well, the dragon is new round here. There were no dragons at all in the river before. We think that the goddess Kuan Yin must have sent him. We'd better go and ask her.'

Now Monkey knew that if Kuan Yin had sent the dragon, this was serious because she was the spirit of all the Buddhas that had ever been in the world, and all that were to come. But how long would the spirits take to get to the far realms where she lived? Perhaps Monkey and Tripitaka would be dead from cold or starvation, or both, before they returned.

'Don't you worry,' a voice from the sky said suddenly. It was the Golden Headed Guardian. 'You all stay where you are. I'll go and find her.'

'Thank you very much,' Monkey answered. 'I'd be very grateful if you'd go at once.'

The Guardian soared back up through the clouds and headed for the Southern Ocean where Kuan Yin, the Goddess of Mercy, resided. He found her sitting peacefully on her lotus seat in a bamboo grove. 'Your Ladyship,' he said, 'Tripitaka, the priest, has lost his horse in Eagle Grief River. It was swallowed up by a dragon.'

'Oh no!' Kuan Yin cried. 'That dragon is meant to help Tripitaka! I put him there on purpose! What's he doing eating the man's horse? I'd better come and sort it out!' So saying, Kuan Yin rose from her lotus seat, left her sacred grove and crossed the Southern Ocean on a beam of magic light.

When she reached Monkey, he was in a roaring bad temper again.

He leaped into the air shouting, 'You're not much good at your job! You call yourself the teacher of the Buddhas and yet you put monsters like this in our path. You should be helping us!'

'You ridiculous, red-bottomed monkey!' Kuan Yin snapped back. 'I've taken a lot of trouble to see Tripitaka safely on his way and also to make you a bit more holy and serious too. And this is all the thanks I get!'

'Don't try and blame me!' said Monkey. 'I would have been only too happy just to amuse myself when I finally got out of that mountain, but no, you would have me go on this dreadful journey. Well, what are we going to do now?'

Kuan Yin laughed. 'Oh, Monkey,' she said, 'we have to keep you busy, or you'd soon be up to your old tricks again. The dragon is meant to offer your master a ride. No ordinary horse could carry him over such difficult ground, you know.'

'That's all very well,' said Monkey grumpily, 'but now he's eaten the horse and won't come out of the river again.'

Kuan Yin ordered the Golden Headed Guardian to go to the edge of the river and cry, 'Third son of the Dragon King, come out!'

'He'll be out fast as lightning — you'll see,' she said. And he was. The dragon appeared immediately from the water and bowed to Kuan Yin.

'Didn't you realise that Monkey is serving the Scripture Seeker on his journey?' asked Kuan Yin.

'No, I didn't,' said the dragon, a little sulkily. 'I was hungry yesterday and ate his horse, and then he fought me because of it. How was I supposed to know who he was? He never said anything about scriptures!'

'You never asked me my name!' retorted Monkey indignantly.

'Oh yes, I did!' said the dragon. 'I asked what kind of horrible monster you were, but you didn't answer. You just complained about your horse!'

'Well, Monkey,' said Kuan Yin, 'you know what to do in future. Always tell people that you're on a pilgrimage to find the scriptures, and then there won't be any more trouble.' But knowing Monkey, she doubted this.

Then she went to the dragon and removed the jewel of wisdom from under his chin. She took her wand of willow leaves and shook it over him, sprinkling him with dew. Then she blew upon him with a magic breath and cried, 'Change!' The dragon at once changed into a horse, exactly like the one that had been eaten!

'Now then,' the goddess said sternly to the dragon-horse. 'Behave yourself, stop eating what doesn't belong to you, and I promise you shall become an enlightened creature with a golden body!'

This is what everyone who follows the Buddha's teachings longs for — the enlightenment which brings complete wisdom about life and death. So the dragon-horse bowed down humbly to Kuan Yin and said that he would do as he was told.

'That's all very well!' said Monkey, grabbing at Kuan Yin rather rudely as she turned to go. 'It's very difficult, you know, travelling to the West. There are dreadful mountains and precipices, and who knows what other monsters we'll meet on the way? No, I'm sorry, but you've got to do better than that!'

'Well, Monkey,' said Kuan Yin, 'in the old days you used to be keen on the idea of enlightenment. Now as soon as things get a little difficult, you want to run back home again. Don't you know that Earth herself will help you when you are in trouble, if you call on her? If necessary, I'll come myself. But I do have something else to give you.'

Taking up her willow wand, she swished the leaves over Monkey's back. 'Change!' she cried again. At once three of the leaves changed into magic hairs. 'There,' she said. 'Take these. They will get you out of any trouble, however bad.'

And, indeed, there were plenty more adventures before Monkey and Tripitaka finally found the precious scriptures and brought them safely back home again.

Dunhuang~ The City of Sands

We've reached Anxi, the town marking the beginning of the Taklamakan Desert. Here you can go left or right around the desert, or even through the middle. But this isn't always a good idea. Many people say that 'Taklamakan' means 'He who goes in, does not come out'.

Travellers have always given special names to places along the Silk Road. Just to the north of the Taklamakan Desert, for instance, are the Celestial Mountains — snow-capped and beautiful. Near Khotan are the Greater and Lesser Headache Mountains, where your head can hurt badly as you climb higher and higher and the air gets thinner and thinner.

Water is a vital resource on the Silk Road. The caravans need to know where their next watering place will be, and the names of the oases give a clue as to the kind of water they offer. One Cup Spring, Bitter Well Halt and Mud Pit Hollow all warn us not to expect too much. Sometimes it's very hard to find the springs, and travellers have to search around for a tiny dip in the ground, marked by a single stone. Even when they find the water, it may be bitter and brackish and not quench their thirst.

If we turned right at Anxi, we could go to the city of Turpan — twelve days' hard travel, with only nasty-tasting water on the way. But in Turpan itself there is delicious cool water. It's brought there through underground channels from the mountains, and flows around the town and its gardens. That's why they can grow such lovely fruit and vegetables there.

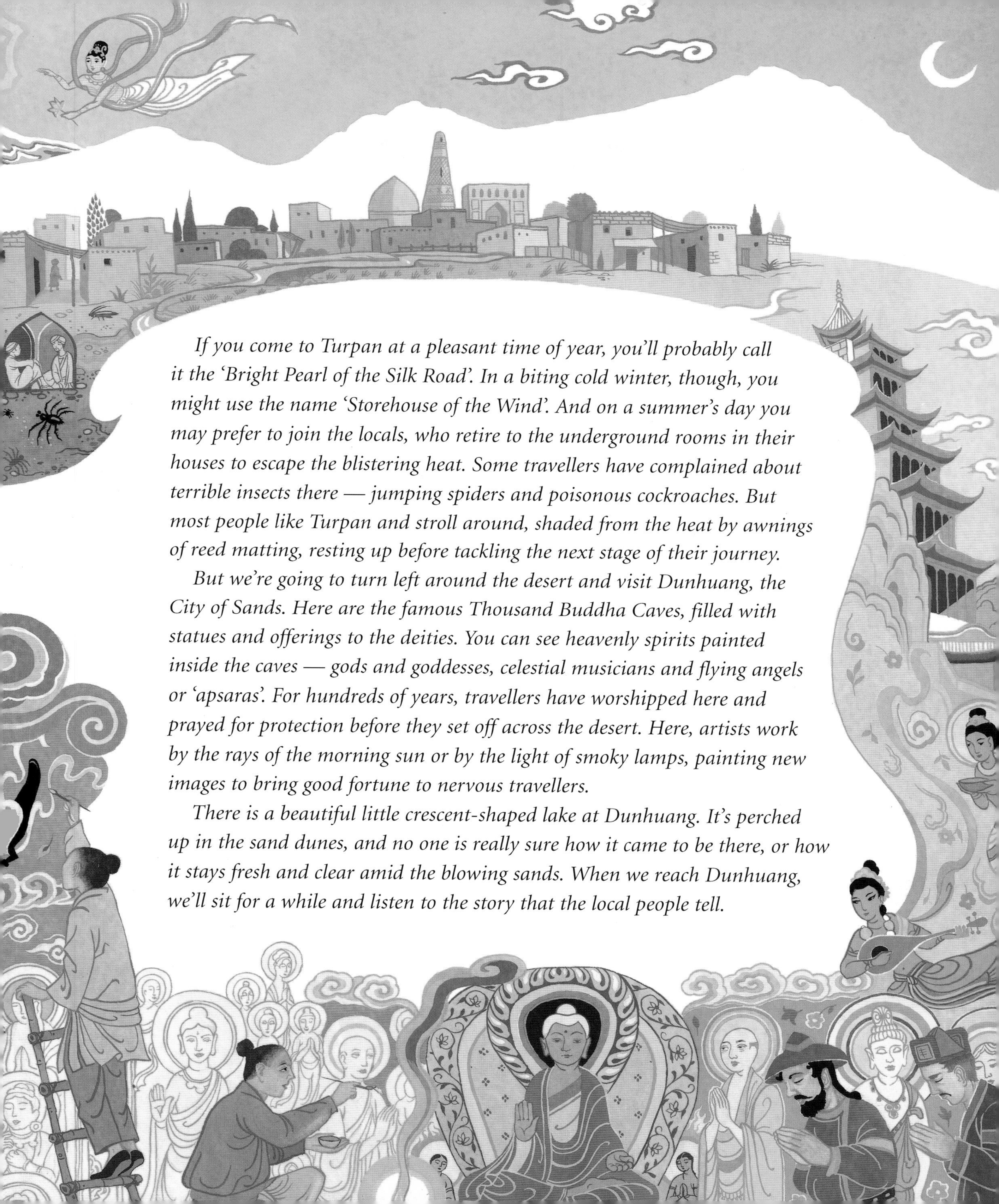

If you come to Turpan at a pleasant time of year, you'll probably call it the 'Bright Pearl of the Silk Road'. In a biting cold winter, though, you might use the name 'Storehouse of the Wind'. And on a summer's day you may prefer to join the locals, who retire to the underground rooms in their houses to escape the blistering heat. Some travellers have complained about terrible insects there — jumping spiders and poisonous cockroaches. But most people like Turpan and stroll around, shaded from the heat by awnings of reed matting, resting up before tackling the next stage of their journey.

But we're going to turn left around the desert and visit Dunhuang, the City of Sands. Here are the famous Thousand Buddha Caves, filled with statues and offerings to the deities. You can see heavenly spirits painted inside the caves — gods and goddesses, celestial musicians and flying angels or 'apsaras'. For hundreds of years, travellers have worshipped here and prayed for protection before they set off across the desert. Here, artists work by the rays of the morning sun or by the light of smoky lamps, painting new images to bring good fortune to nervous travellers.

There is a beautiful little crescent-shaped lake at Dunhuang. It's perched up in the sand dunes, and no one is really sure how it came to be there, or how it stays fresh and clear amid the blowing sands. When we reach Dunhuang, we'll sit for a while and listen to the story that the local people tell.

White Cloud Fairy

Once there was almost nothing at Dunhuang. Where now you see houses and streets, people and donkeys, there was just sand and scrubby bushes.

But the land was not quite empty. Nearby, some people were living at a small oasis by the foot of the Sanwei Mountain. Here life was very hard, and they had to struggle with frequent droughts and sand-storms which often threatened to destroy their meagre harvests. They managed to survive, however, until a year came when the drought was worse than any before. No rain fell at all and the oasis began to dry up.

Day after day people went out to their fields hoping for some kind of a miracle, but all they saw were their crops turning brown under the burning rays of the sun. Around their homes the trees they had planted for shade began to shed their leaves until their branches were black and bare. The people shook with fear, for they knew they were doomed unless water appeared from somewhere.

'And what do you expect from up there?' asked one old man bitterly, when he saw a young woman gazing hopefully upwards. As usual there was not a cloud in the sky. 'Do you think they're going to throw open the gates of Heaven and pour down pitchers of water for us?'

The young woman looked at him angrily. It wasn't so bad for him, for he had lived a good long life already. But she had three small children. How could she bear to see them suffer? Without water they would all soon die. She said another prayer to Heaven, and put all her love and anguish into that prayer.

And, quite by chance, someone did hear her. Just one white cloud came gently drifting by in that bright blue sky, and it happened to be the White Cloud Fairy. When she heard the poor woman's words, they cut her heart like a knife. She wanted to help but she didn't see how she could. She couldn't make rain without permission from the Dragon King or assistance from the Thunder God. She couldn't ask the Dragon King because he was having a rest and snapped crossly at anyone who disturbed him. And the Thunder God had gone off to play in the western mountains where he could make his booming voice roll all around their rocky slopes. He thought it funny to frighten people and watch them run away.

So what could she do? The poor woman below was crying now, and at the sound of her sobs White Cloud Fairy burst into tears too.

But her bright silvery tears weren't like salty earth tears at all. They fell to the ground in huge drops and began to collect into a puddle. White Cloud Fairy cried and cried because she hadn't really cried about anything for a long time and had plenty of tears saved up. Ever since she was a young wisp of a White Cloud Fairy, she could never stop crying easily once she had started. So her tears kept on falling until the little puddle became a bright pool on the ground.

The young woman was so astonished that she stopped crying. She had to step back as the drops splashed down faster than ever! The pool became so deep that a bubbling spring arose in the middle of it. And from out of the pool flowed a stream, which ran first with a trickle, then a gurgle, and then in a great rush across the parched ground.

Other people had gathered round to look. 'I've never seen anything like it!' exclaimed one man. 'All that water out of one cloud. Heaven's playing tricks on us again!'

'If these are Heaven's tricks, then I welcome them every time,' said the young woman whose prayer had been answered.

Laughing, skipping and running, people sped off down the street to fetch their buckets to fill with water and their tools to dig the fields.

Soon everything was looking wonderful again. The grain was ripening, the fruit was growing plump, the leaves were green again on the trees. The people decided to build a splendid temple in honour of White Cloud Fairy. She would now be the chief goddess in their land. They made a beautiful statue of her and covered it with gold. When everything was ready, they crowded into the temple and began to light incense and say prayers to thank White Cloud Fairy for her kindness.

What the people had forgotten, though, was that they already had another temple, just over the road. This was built for the Sand God, and until now they had said their prayers to him. It paid to keep on the right side of the Sand God, because he could make life very difficult, with dreadful sandstorms that could swallow up whole villages.

Like the Thunder God, the Sand God had also been away in the west. His favourite game was to make shapes in the desert, raising new sand dunes and smoothing them into beautiful curves. On the way home, he had a bit of extra fun when he covered a little settlement of houses with sand. The people there hadn't been saying their prayers to him often enough. No one was allowed to forget about the Sand God for long! Luckily for them, they saw the sandstorm coming and ran away from their houses just in time. But now they would have to spend weeks digging out their homes.

So when the Sand God got back to his home at Sanwei Mountain and saw the bright new temple built for White Cloud Fairy, he was furious! What was she doing here? And why had nobody consulted him? There was almost nothing in his own temple — no offerings of fruit, scarcely a stick of incense and only a couple of old women muttering their prayers. He looked over the road and saw the crowds around the gorgeous golden statue of White Cloud Fairy and decided that something had to be done.

The Sand God flew into a terrible rage. He stamped his feet and shouted angrily, 'White Cloud Fairy, this is my place, not yours! How dare you spill out your useless tears here and make all these stupid people worship you! Now we'll see which of us is really more powerful! Just watch this!'

He picked up a handful of sand and scattered it over the edge of the stream shouting, 'Rise!'

At once a great mountain of sand rose all around and began to block up the spring of water. First the brave, bubbling spring slowed down to a trickle, then it died away completely.

People tore at their hair and clothes in despair. 'The Drought Monster has come back and drunk up all our water!' they cried. They didn't understand what the real problem was.

White Cloud Fairy heard the commotion and flew over to see what was going on. She knew at once where the trouble lay. 'That's the Sand God,' she said to herself crossly when she saw the huge mountain of sand. 'Perhaps I can use my own magic to work against his — but no, that wouldn't be allowed. This is his place. What happened before with my tears was an accident. So what can I do to help now?'

White Cloud Fairy bowed her head in thought for a moment, then raised it triumphantly. 'I know! I'll fly up to the highest place of all, the Ninth Heaven, and ask for help.'

The Goddess of the Ninth Heaven met her at the gates and led her into her palace, saying, 'It must be something rather important to bring you all the way up here.'

When they were seated in the palace, White Cloud Fairy asked the Goddess respectfully, 'May I borrow something from you?'

'What exactly do you have in mind?' asked the Goddess.

'I'd like to borrow the moon,' said White Cloud Fairy.

'The moon! What do you want with her?'

'The Sand God has bullied me and is making life miserable for the people down below.' When White Cloud Fairy had explained everything to the Goddess, she said, 'I've thought of a plan, though, and if you'll lend me the moon, I've got a good chance of making my idea work.'

'Very well,' said the Goddess. 'I can see that you've been trying to help the people, so I ought to give you my support. But the trouble is, the moon is only in her fifth day at the moment. She's not very rounded yet.'

It was early in the lunar month and the moon herself was just a delectable, delicate crescent — a silver sliver of light.

'Never mind,' said White Cloud Fairy. 'That'll do nicely.'

She took the shining crescent in both hands and flew down again swiftly. In front of her temple she spread the moon out carefully on the ground. Before you could blink an eye, the moon had turned into a crystal lake with little rippling waves. And, of course, the lake itself was the lovely crescent shape of the young moon.

Everybody gasped and clapped. White Cloud Fairy had done it again!

'We'll call it Crescent Moon Lake,' someone shouted.

'Yes! Crescent Moon Lake!' And they all clapped even louder.

The Sand God was now rasping with rage, which was as near as he could get to foaming at the mouth. He blew the sand as fiercely as he could into the lake, trying to fill it up.

But when the Goddess saw this, she just laughed from her palace in the Ninth Heaven and waved her long silken sleeves so that a gentle breeze sprang up and carried all the sand away again.

Soon the Sand God realised that he was wasting his breath. Snarling, he retired, and the sweet waters of Crescent Moon Lake stretched out peacefully again.

Then the Goddess put another tiny sliver of light back in the sky, so that the moon above could look down and smile when she saw herself reflected in the curved crescent of water below. Whenever the Sand God tried his tricks again, the Goddess would once more set her sleeves of silk billowing till the sand flew up towards the top of the dune.

Even today you can hear the roaring of the sands when the Sand God is in a bad mood. And you may even see the sand blowing uphill when the Goddess of the Ninth Heaven rustles her sleeves, as she always does, to keep it away from the Crescent Moon Lake at Dunhuang.

Demons & Dragons of the Taklamakan

We're passing through the desert now, moving on from one oasis city to the next. It's not only the desert that the caravans fear, but robbers too. Everyone knows that they're prowling around, looking for parties of travellers to attack. They have local spies who tell them when a choice load of goods is coming their way. People say that robbers on the Silk Road are magicians, too, and can cast a spell of darkness over a caravan so that it falls into their clutches.

But stay with me; you'll be safe. My silken threads will quickly whisk us out of any trouble! Most caravans travel by night because it's cooler then. Their leaders have learned to read their way by the stars. It's important that everyone leaves together, so a call is given about three hours before sunset, to wake people up in time for the night's travel. And a signpost is put up so that anyone who oversleeps has the chance to catch up.

It doesn't always work, though. Look — there are some bleached bones lying on the ground. They're probably those of travellers who got lost in the desert. And you must be careful; there are terrible demons and spirits who can lead you astray. They call out to you, like old friends, and lead you off course. When you're trying to look for your caravan, you may hear the tramp of hundreds of feet in the distance and hurry off to join your people. But you'll only find yourself lost and alone in the burning sands of the desert — and the demons, laughing with glee, will have all disappeared. The desert

plays tricks on your eyesight too. You might glimpse a cool oasis or march towards a distant city. And, suddenly, there's nothing — it was all a mirage.

At the eastern end of the Taklamakan Desert is a dreadful deserted place called Lop Nor, which the great traveller Marco Polo struggled to cross on his way to Dunhuang. Once there was a thriving city there, called Loulan, but the lake nearby dried up into a salty marsh and the place, so travellers say, has become haunted by demons and dragons. Indeed, everywhere in the desert are spirits who can whip up terrible sand-storms. We heard a little about them at Dunhuang. Even in a walled city, sand can suddenly rain down from the sky and all the inhabitants perish miserably under it. There are many such lost cities in the Taklamakan. They say that the city of Katak was swallowed up by sand in only a few hours because its inhabitants had forgotten how to pray properly. Now do you see why travellers were making their prayers and offerings to the Buddha at Dunhuang?

But now we've reached another oasis. You can see groups of merchants huddled up together for safety. They've come from far-off countries and cities both from the East and the West. A merchant from Persia has a story to tell. It's just right for this place, but I'm not sure it'll cheer up his companions!

The Enchanted Garden

IT WAS THE NIGHT OF THE FULL MOON, when young Mahan went off to a party with his friends. He was fond of merry-making and much too fond of drinking, and by the time they had left one party and gone to a second, and a third, his head was in a whirl.

'I need some fresh air!' he told himself and wandered off unsteadily into a grove of palm trees. 'Oh, what a beautiful moon!' he cried, holding up his arms to the sky.

'My friend,' said a deep voice, very close to him. Mahan nearly jumped out of his skin. A man was standing right next to him. By his clothes, he looked like a well-to-do merchant.

'I hope you can help me. I have a caravan waiting to come into the city. It's laden with the choicest goods, and I will let you share my profits if you can help me get it into the city tonight. You see, the gates are closed already and the guards won't let me in. But you are a man of the town, I can tell, and I'm sure you can persuade them.'

'Oh!' Mahan was taken by surprise. 'I don't know. I too have to stay out here until they open the gates at first light. But — share your profits, did you say?'

The stranger nodded eagerly. 'Oh yes! You will have bags and bags of gold. But if my caravan has to stay out here all night, I'm afraid that robbers will come and make off with the goods.'

Bags and bags of gold! Gold coins danced and shone in front of Mahan's eyes as he imagined all this. 'Yes, I'll try to help you!' he said.

'Good!' said the merchant. 'Follow me.'

He set off at a very fast pace, and Mahan had to jog along to keep up. On and on they went for hours, until Mahan lost all sense of direction.

Then the first light of dawn glimmered in the sky and Mahan looked around him. The merchant was nowhere to be seen. But Mahan was so tired that he lay down on the ground and fell into a deep, deep sleep.

When he awoke, the glaring rays of the midday sun were beating down upon him. He sat up. Where was he? All around him was barren desert. Here and there were rocky outcrops, but when he looked for shade among them, he saw that they were riddled with small caves and every cave was writhing with hissing serpents.

Mahan walked on, parched and hungry, but he found nothing. It was only as evening drew on that he saw two figures in the distance. He ran to meet them. They were an old couple, a man and woman with kind, wrinkled faces, walking arm in arm through the desert.

'Dear Father and Mother!' Mahan called to them. 'Help me, please! I'm lost.' And he told them the story of how he had come to this place.

They looked very grave. 'Oh dear,' said the old woman at last, 'I'm afraid you've been deceived. That merchant was a demon of the desert and led you into his kingdom of demons. But follow us and you'll be safe. Just listen to these magic words and they'll protect you.'

With that, she whispered some secret words in his ear. Mahan trudged along after the pair all night, and then as dawn broke once more, he saw a welcoming sight: no desert, but green and growing land. Just ahead of him was a village, with smoke rising from the early baking, chickens and goats wandering the streets, and people watering their gardens.

The sky was still misty, with the promise of a fine day. Mahan clapped his hands for joy. He began to run towards the village. But as he came closer to it, the mist thickened. He couldn't see the village any more. He kept going in the same direction, until suddenly the mist cleared again. Mahan stopped and blinked. There was no village. He had been tricked again! He tried reciting the magic words the old woman had taught him, but they did nothing at all. In fact, there was nothing around him except bare rocks.

He was standing all alone in a rocky gorge. Desperate for something to eat and drink, he began to dig in the crevices between the rocks, scrabbling with his fingers until they bled. At last he found some dry roots and chewed on these.

Then there was a ring of hooves on the rocks. Looking up, he saw a horseman riding towards him and leading a second horse.

'What are you doing?' the horseman asked Mahan, and Mahan told him about his adventures.

'I'm afraid you were deceived,' said the horseman. 'They were no ordinary old couple — they were demons, and their words put a spell on you. But never mind! Climb on this horse and we'll get out of here.'

As they rode through the rocky gorge, Mahan could hear a faint but strange noise coming towards him, like a kind of wild music. The noise got louder and louder until suddenly, round a corner, he nearly collided with a procession of monsters! They were more horrible than anything he could have imagined.

Each one had the trunk of an elephant, the horns of an ox and a nasty, slimy skin. Each one carried a torch in its fearsome mouth, and yet they could all still keep up a terrible din. Mahan's horse reared up, and then it changed under him into a huge, scaly dragon, with seven heads, great leathery wings and a spiky, lashing tail.

Mahan was nearly paralysed with terror. He tried to jump off, but too late! The dragon shrieked and soared up into the air, its wings beating fiercely. Mahan became so giddy that he couldn't see where they were going, but he clung on as best he could to the dragon's sharp scales. Darkness descended and they flew on and on through the night.

When the first rays of the morning sun were striking the distant hills, they came down to earth. The dragon threw Mahan roughly on to the ground, scratching him viciously with its claws. Mahan was almost too tired to care. Sore and weary, he fell into a deep sleep.

When he awoke, a more pleasant sight greeted his eyes. He was lying in a cool orchard. Above him stretched out the inviting boughs of a peach tree, laden with fruit. Mahan leaped up and seized a peach. Parched with thirst, he crammed it into his mouth, the juice running down his chin.

'Hey, you! What do you think you're doing, stealing my peaches?' An old man came running at him, waving a stick.

'Oh, forgive me, please!' said Mahan through a mouthful of peach. And he told the old man how desperately he needed to eat and drink.

'My poor young friend!' said the old man. 'Of course you may eat as much as you like! And take your rest here too.'

He shook a branch or two so that more luscious peaches tumbled down at Mahan's feet. Then, stroking his beard thoughtfully, he made Mahan a proposal.

'I have no son,' he said, 'and now suddenly you are here. It seems like a gift from God. So how about if I make you my heir? Everything that I have will be yours when I die.'

Mahan couldn't believe his good fortune. He agreed eagerly.

'There's just one condition,' said the old man. 'You must spend one night in this orchard, and you must keep silent all night. You'll sit up in that tree, and you won't say a word. Agreed?'

Mahan nodded happily. It was a strange thing to ask, but who wouldn't agree, in return for inheriting such a fine orchard?

So when night came, Mahan climbed up into the tree to sit there silently until dawn. He was still very tired after his adventures, and it wasn't long before he nodded off. Slowly the moon rose, and when he awoke, suddenly the orchard was radiant with beautiful, silvery light.

But it wasn't the moon that had woken him. Down there below him he saw a troop of fairies enjoying a banquet. And among them was their queen — the loveliest creature that Mahan had ever set eyes on. As he peered down at them in astonishment, the fairies looked up and laughed. Then they beckoned him down to join them.

Mahan forgot all about his promise to be silent and enjoyed himself with the fairies all night. They ate delicious fairy food and sipped nectar from silver goblets. Sometimes the fairies danced to delightful music which filled the orchard with its delicate sound. But, most of all, Mahan was enchanted by the exquisite fairy queen. All night they sat together and talked of love.

As the moon began to sink in the sky, Mahan reached out to embrace his beloved. Suddenly he was no longer holding the queen in his arms, but a horrible monster! It was a hideous creature, yet he couldn't get away; until day dawned, he was locked in her grip and had to suffer her loathsome caresses!

When the sun rose, he found himself alone again but no longer in that fine, shady orchard. No, he was out in the burning desert once again, with only blackened stumps to show where the trees had been. Mahan wept bitterly. How could he have been such a fool?

'I have been tempted by gold and false promises,' he said. 'I have been greedy and reckless. I couldn't even keep my word! I deserve everything I have been made to suffer!'

At that moment a man dressed in green appeared quietly before him. Mahan was terrified — it must be another demon come to torment him!

'Don't be frightened, my good friend Mahan,' said the man. 'I am the Khizr, the Green Messenger, sent by God himself. Put your trust in God, and in me as his helper, and I will save you. Close your eyes and let me take your hand.'

Mahan recognised at once the goodness and truth in the stranger's eyes, now that he was no longer blinded by greed. He did as he was told, and the Khizr in green led him safely back to the grove of trees where he had first met the evil merchant.

When Mahan opened his eyes, he shouted for joy. His friends were there too — but what was this? They were dressed in mourning robes, for they thought that Mahan was dead and gone. Their tears soon turned to rejoicing, though, and they all embraced one another thankfully.

Mahan promised himself that he would always wear mourning robes from now on, to remind him of what a fool he had been and how the good Khizr had saved him. Until the end of his days Mahan led a happy and useful life. Never again did he have any trouble with demons!

Kashgar Caravanserai

We have left the desert behind us now and climbed up to the ancient city of Kashgar. This is a real crossroads, where the folk of the mountain and the plain meet. We'll see all sorts of people in the market. Over there are some weary traders from China who have reached the end of their journey. They will sell their goods and will go home with a new load. Here are some merchants from far-off Samarkand — sharp-eyed, richly dressed, always ready to spot a bargain. Over there are two Buddhist monks from India, carrying scrolls from one monastery to another. Those rosy-cheeked, black-eyed girls are Tajiks, and you might spot a few fair heads among the dark-haired people from the Hindu Kush. Some of their ancestors were Greeks, who came with the army of Alexander the Great. The locals here are the Uighurs. They manage the trade routes skilfully. The older men among them like to grow long grey beards.

You might wonder how all these people manage to understand each other. But many of them speak one of the Turkic languages, which have a common root, so it's just about possible. The first person begins by saying something like, 'I'm going to speak about sheep today,' so that the second person knows what the conversation will be about.

People often grumble about taxes. Greedy rulers and officials along the Silk Road charge the caravans 'protection' or 'duty' and if you don't pay up, your goods won't go any further. No wonder the price of silk is hundreds of times higher in the West than in China!

In the bigger places, most travellers stay at an inn or 'caravanserai', with a courtyard for the animals, usually two-humped camels, which can travel for long periods without water and food. Horses are useful too, for fast travel over shorter distances. Mules and donkeys can carry heavy loads in the mountains, and you'll also see yaks, which are at home in the highlands. Caravans have to change their pack animals when they tire, and lots of arguing goes on as the team drivers bargain for the best replacements.

People also stock up on provisions. Those going west need warm wraps, sheepskins and furs for the hard climb into the snowy mountains. There are harsh times ahead; they may suffer fierce blizzards and altitude sickness. Pack animals may tumble over the edge of a precipice, and nights may be spent shivering on a mat laid down on the ice.

Some caravans wait here for months until the highest mountain passes open again. When they get bored, they scratch poems and messages on the walls of the inns — like this one:

Jewels and gems, they are but stones;
Barley and beans, they strengthen your bones.

When you're suffering from cold and hunger, you don't care much for your precious cargo. You'd trade it all in for a bowl of warm gruel!

Over there are some shepherds from the mountains of Afghanistan. Let's follow them to the caravanserai and hear the stories they're telling today.

THE MAGIC SADDLEBAG

HIGH UP IN THE MOUNTAINS OF THE HINDU KUSH lived three brothers called Masud, Hamid and Wali. Their parents had died when they were little, and they had lived together on their own since then. Now that they had grown up into young men, they decided to leave the village and seek their fortunes, going wherever their journey took them. The caravan drivers who passed by had told them about the long roads snaking up through mountain passes and down into hidden valleys filled with sweet apricots and flowers. The brothers had also heard how kings ruled in splendid palaces, where feasts were held for thousands of guests, and were determined to see these wonders for themselves.

One day, an old mule-driver passed by the boys' home. As they were talking, he said,'Yes, lads, go seek your fortunes. But always have your eyes and ears open for the signs God sends you along the way. And remember — take what you are given, and no more. Be ready to help others, and you will be helped too.'

The brothers set out, travelling for many days up difficult mountain paths, and down into unknown lands. When they reached the plains, they decided to rest for a while. Exhausted, all three brothers fell into a deep sleep.

Masud, the eldest, had the strangest dream. He heard bells ringing and a voice which said to him, 'Masud! Masud! Dig down into the ground below and you will find gold!'

Masud woke up with a start. It was just daybreak and he began to dig at once. The other brothers thought he was mad. But there were pieces of gold in the earth, and Masud soon filled his pockets with them.

'Well, that's enough for me!' he said joyfully. 'I've enough gold here to build myself a decent house and marry a pretty wife. That's my journey over with. Brothers, I bid you farewell!' And Masud set off for home.

Hamid and Wali were pleased at his good fortune, but sorry to part with him. They trudged on together till they came to a great forest. Here they lay down to sleep under a huge tree. In the night Hamid had a strange dream. He heard trumpets blowing loudly and a voice calling out to him, 'Hamid! Hamid! Dig down in the ground below and you will find jewels!'

He woke up, and as it was already morning he began to dig at once. Just like Masud before him, he soon struck lucky. He pulled out a large pot, full to the brim with precious stones of every kind.

'Look, Wali! Fortune has smiled on me too, and my journey has come to an end. I want nothing more than to go home, build myself a fine house and marry a handsome girl from the village. So, goodbye!'

'Now what do I do?' said Wali to himself. 'Has God forgotten about me? Why is my journey so long and theirs so short?' But he remembered that everyone has a different path and a different fate. Bravely he picked up his bundle and plunged into the forest. He had nothing left to eat or drink now, and in the dense, dark forest he soon began to feel afraid. 'I'll climb up this tree,' he thought, 'and see if I can glimpse anything ahead.'

He climbed right to the top, but whichever way he looked there was nothing but forest. 'Perhaps it's my fate to die here,' he said to himself sadly.

But when he climbed down again, there on the ground lay a beautifully embroidered saddlebag. How could it have got there? Perhaps there was something to eat inside! Wali picked the saddlebag up hopefully and opened it. But there was nothing inside, nothing at all.

'Well, this must be my bit of luck — and what bad luck it is too!' he exclaimed. 'Masud finds gold, Hamid gets a pot of jewels and all I get is an empty saddlebag. Oh, how I wish it was full of food for me to eat!'

He was about to throw the empty saddlebag away in disgust, when suddenly he noticed that it was now full — full to bursting with delicious food! Eagerly he unpacked it and found roast chicken, ripe fruit, fresh bread and cheese, and iced sherbet to drink. Wali began to eat and eat. When he had finished, he wiped his mouth and said to himself thoughtfully, 'I suppose this is a magic saddlebag. Will it grant me other wishes, I wonder? Look at my clothes! They're almost in rags now. I'd love a new suit and some boots would be nice!'

No sooner had he said this than the saddlebag was full again. He pulled out a fur-lined jacket, some smart woollen trousers and a pair of fine leather boots, all just the right size for him.

Wali was about to wish for all sorts of other things which he didn't really need, when he remembered the words of the old mule-driver. 'I'd better not be greedy,' he thought.

So he travelled on, asking for meals from the magic saddlebag whenever he was hungry. He travelled for six days through the mighty forest, until at last he saw fields and orchards ahead of him. 'I'll be glad to have some human company again! I'm quite tired of talking to myself,' he said.

He approached a little house set in a pretty garden and knocked boldly on the door. A small, fat woman, dressed all in black, answered it.

'Greetings, Mother,' he said. 'Could you give me shelter for the night? I've been on the road for many days now. My two brothers have already found their fortunes, but I'm still seeking mine.'

'Certainly, young man,' the woman replied. 'You're very welcome. My son is about your age, and he'll be happy to have you as a companion. But have you really found nothing yet on your travels?'

She looked at him with sharp curiosity, and Wali felt obliged to show her his saddlebag. 'Only this old thing,' he said. 'It was quite empty when I found it.' He didn't want to tell her anything about its magic powers.

Soon her son came home from his work in the fields, and the woman gave the two young men their supper. They were eating the rice and vegetables, when the woman suddenly said, 'Oh no! I forgot to get the meat for you! How could I be so stupid?'

'Don't worry,' said Wali, 'I can get you some meat.' He secretly wished for just enough meat for the three of them, and this is exactly what he pulled out of the saddlebag. The young man and his mother were amazed. 'Are you some kind of a magician?' the mother cried.

Wali bit his lip. He had only wanted to help, but now he was rather sorry that he'd made the wish. 'No, I'm not a magician, just an ordinary man like your son here. The saddlebag is a special one, though.'

And he said no more, although they pressed him to say how he found it, and what it would do for him.

When Wali went to bed that night, the young man was determined to get his hands on the saddlebag. He crept over to where Wali lay on the kitchen floor in front of the warm oven and picked up the saddlebag. He shook it out eagerly, but there was nothing inside.

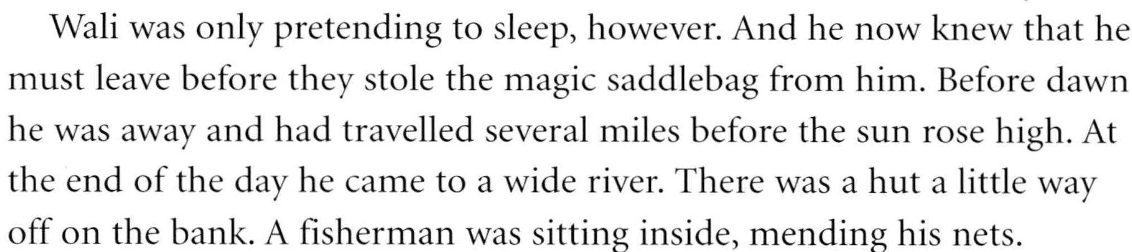

Wali was only pretending to sleep, however. And he now knew that he must leave before they stole the magic saddlebag from him. Before dawn he was away and had travelled several miles before the sun rose high. At the end of the day he came to a wide river. There was a hut a little way off on the bank. A fisherman was sitting inside, mending his nets.

'Hello, Father!' said Wali.

The fisherman was very surprised. 'And good day to you too, stranger. We don't get many visitors in these parts. What brings you here?'

'I was travelling with my two brothers, seeking our fortunes,' said Wali. 'They have found theirs, but I'm still searching for mine. May I sleep in your hut tonight? It's getting very late.'

'Of course,' said the fisherman. 'It'll be a pleasure to hear your story. It's a long time since I have had a visitor.'

When they had eaten a simple meal, the fisherman told Wali about his greatest sorrow. 'My dear wife has been stolen from me,' he said. 'Not long ago robbers came here looking for money, and when they couldn't find any, they took my wife away with them. They want me to buy her back, but all I have in the world is in this bare hut.'

Here was someone who really needed his help, thought Wali. So he whispered into the saddlebag, 'Return the fisherman's wife!' And suddenly, there she was, stepping out of the bag, blinking with surprise.

The fisherman could not believe his eyes. 'Are you a conjuror?' he asked.

'No!' said Wali. 'My saddlebag is a little bit unusual, but I'm an ordinary man, just like you.' And he created a magnificent feast to celebrate the wife's return, with the help, of course, of the magic saddlebag.

The next morning, when he went outside to wash in the river, he heard the couple talking in the hut.

'You must get hold of that young man's saddlebag!' the wife was saying to her husband. 'Just think — we could be rich! Wonderful food and clothes whenever we want, and chests full of silver and gold!'

Wali realised that they would try to trick him out of his saddlebag. Luckily he had brought it with him — he never went anywhere without it now — so he left straight away. The path was rugged and led uphill over steep rocks and the day grew hotter and hotter. Wali's feet were sore and he badly wanted to rest. But suddenly he heard a voice calling from the bushes, 'Help! Help! Please, God, let someone hear me!'

Under the bushes, Wali found a girl lying tied up on the ground. Her clothes were in rags and she had no shoes on her feet. Wali quickly took a knife to the ropes and set her free. At first the girl could hardly speak, she was so hoarse, but after a drink of water she recovered a little; she told him that her name was Zuleika.

'My father took a new wife,' she whispered, 'and she hated me. She sent me away to another house, where they kept me like a slave. I ran away, but some robbers captured me, and left me here to die. Please, take me to my father!' she begged. 'I know he'll reward you!'

'Of course I will,' said Wali, 'but perhaps we should get some new clothes for you first.'

He whispered into the magic saddlebag and pulled out a pair of pink silk trousers, a velvet tunic of deep red, some golden slippers and a gossamer veil. When Zuleika put them on, she looked like a young princess.

Wali and Zuleika set out together and it wasn't long before they saw a fine large house, with orchards around it.

'This is my home,' said Zuleika. 'But I must cover my face with the veil so that no one recognises me.'

The servant who opened the door was suspicious but led them into her father's study. At first Zuleika's father thought they were strangers, but when she threw back her veil, he wept with joy.

'Oh, my daughter!' he said. 'Your stepmother told me you had drowned in the lake!'

When he heard how cruelly her stepmother had treated her, he flew into a rage and threw the wicked woman out of the house at once.

'You are most welcome to stay here with us,' he said to Wali. 'I can never thank you enough for what you've done!'

Wali agreed, for as he looked into Zuleika's beautiful eyes, he knew that his fortune was found and he need travel the world no more. Wali and Zuleika were married, and they lived together happily for the rest of their lives. They could ask the magic saddlebag for whatever they needed. And because they asked it for just enough and no more, it went on serving them faithfully till the end of their days.

Heavenly Horses of the Kirghiz

We're passing through Kirghiz country now. We're high up in the mountains, but even higher above us, snowy peaks glisten in the sun and eagles circle in the deep blue sky. Here there are grassy highland pastures, studded with little flowers, and streams rush down from the steep slopes bringing clear water for the horses and flocks to drink. Let's pause for a while with this group of Kirghiz nomads. Come into one of the yurts. A yurt is a kind of round, felt tent, stretched over a framework of poles and lattice, that can easily be moved from place to place. Inside, it's very snug, with colourful felt hangings and rugs. There's a little stove to keep it warm and a hole in the roof for the smoke to escape through. We'll refresh ourselves with a drink of sharp-tasting 'kumiss' — that's fermented mare's milk. Then, when dusk falls, we'll sit round and listen to the stories that the Kirghiz tell. They love to swap tales and songs with travellers on the Silk Road.

They've got a great tale of their own, about their hero, Manas. That takes a lot of telling, though; it's so long that even when it's recited for several days at a wedding, the guests still don't get to hear the end of it. Manas was a powerful warrior who fought many battles for the Kirghiz people. Like many peoples along the Silk Road, the Kirghiz have had to fight off invaders, and they've moved about to different places.

They're splendid riders, and men, women and children are all at home on horseback. The Kirghiz saddlecloths are decorated with felt patterns, and their horses are swift and sleek. Horses have always been important on the

Silk Road, and horse trading goes on all the way along it. When the Chinese first found out what fine horses there were in Central Asia, they were very jealous. They had only slow, stocky ponies. They heard that the horses from Kokand, in the Ferghana Valley, were the best of all. In the year 102 BC, the Emperor Wu sent an expedition from China to capture some of these Heavenly Horses. Not surprisingly, the locals weren't keen to give up their mounts and they beat off the Chinese army. But the Chinese soldiers arrived a second time and captured enough horses to take home, though, sadly, many died on the long journey back.

'Khans' are the local lords round here, and when the pilgrim Xuanzang came this way in the seventh century, he met the Great Khan at his winter headquarters just north of Lake Issyk Kul. The Khan wore a robe of green satin and his long hair was bound round with a silken band. He was attended by two hundred officers and countless troops mounted on horses and camels. The Khan took the pilgrim off to a feast in his magnificent pavilion — a kind of giant yurt — embroidered with gold flowers. All his court wore bright silk robes and they tucked into huge mounds of mutton and veal. Xuanzang was a vegetarian but fortunately he was allowed to eat rice cakes, cream, honey and raisins instead.

Evening's coming on now, so let's join the Kirghiz and sit together in one of the cosy yurts. The smoke may get in your eyes a little, but I think you'll hardly notice this when you start listening to one of their stories.

CLEVER ASHIK

AMONG THE KIRGHIZ PEOPLE age is much respected. A really wise old man is called an 'aksakal'. Aksakals like to sit around stroking their beards and discussing what they think is best for everybody. Of course, aksakals are indeed experienced and wise, but they often forget that younger people can be clever too. For a long time, nobody under the age of sixty could possibly be called an aksakal. Then Ashik changed all that.

Ashik had grown up almost on his own, because his mother and father had died when he was little. As soon as he could work for a living, a rich local master — a 'bei' — paid the young boy to look after his flock of sheep. He didn't pay Ashik very much, just enough to keep him in food and shelter and some rough but warm clothing to keep out the bitter mountain winds.

Most of the time, Ashik stayed up in the high pastures with his sheep. But sometimes he came down to the village, usually when the bei wanted to count up his sheep and make sure that Ashik hadn't been cheating

him. On one of these days, when Ashik was walking to the village, he suddenly noticed a frog with a broken leg lying in the road. Maybe a horse had kicked it. He picked it up carefully and took it with him to his hut. There he bandaged up the frog's leg so that it could begin to heal.

Very soon the bei appeared at Ashik's hut, eager to know how many new lambs he had in his flock. He was furious when he saw the frog lying in a shallow pool in a corner of the sheep pen.

'What's the meaning of this?' he asked angrily. 'How dare you dig up my land and waste my time looking after a stupid frog! Don't forget who gives you the money to buy food. Without me you'd be dead by now!'

He began to thrash Ashik with a whip. 'That'll teach you a lesson! You get rid of that filthy, slimy frog at once — do you hear?'

Ashik knew better than to argue. He picked up the frog and took it to a nearby lake. Luckily the frog was now well enough to swim. As it began to move away, it suddenly spoke to him.

'Thank you, Ashik,' it said. 'You've saved my life. Now I'd like to do something for you. Here — this is the best that I can give you.'

And with that, the frog spat out a small green pebble. 'It's a magic pebble,' it explained to Ashik. 'Just rub it when you're in trouble and it will do whatever you ask.'

The frog swam away and Ashik put the pebble carefully in his pocket. On his way back to the village, a horseman galloped past, calling out urgently to him, but Ashik couldn't hear exactly what he said.

When Ashik caught up with him in the village, everybody was in a state of panic. Women were crying, men were shouting and children were running around with no one looking after them. In the middle of the noisy crowd sat the circle of aksakals, whose job it was to decide what to do in a crisis.

Karakhan, a khan who lived nearby, was planning to ruin them all. Every child in the village knew his name, for when they were naughty, their mothers said to them, 'Karakhan will come to get you if you don't behave!'

And now it was true. Karakhan was demanding that the people in their village and in all the villages round about should surrender to him and become his slaves. Some of the neighbouring villagers had already tried to soften his heart by sending messengers to him with gifts, but none of the messengers had returned.

'Perhaps we should try one more time,' the aksakals suggested.

The horseman shook his head. 'It's no good. Karakhan is making impossible conditions. He says that he will only speak to someone who comes not on horseback, not on a camel, not on foot, not through the fields and not along the road.'

The aksakals muttered together further, but they had no solution to offer.

'Let me go!' said Ashik suddenly.

'You?' exclaimed their leader. 'Impudent boy! What can you do against the mighty khan?'

The other aksakals thought that it was very funny, and slapped their sides, chuckling wheezily.

'Listen, please, O Wise Ones,' said Ashik. 'I can do what he asks. I won't ride a horse or a camel or go on foot — I'll ride a goat! And I won't go on the road or across the field. I'll ride on the edge of the road, which is neither.'

The aksakals fell silent. Then their faces brightened. Yes, they liked the idea! So Ashik set off, riding the oldest goat in the village and leading a tall camel as a present for the greedy khan.

When Karakhan saw Ashik approaching him like this, he let out a roar of fury. 'You cheeky young brat! Why have you come here, riding a filthy old goat? You should be crawling towards me on your knees!'

'I am only trying to follow your instructions,' said Ashik respectfully. 'I haven't come to you on a horse, or a camel, or on foot. And, as you saw for yourself, I rode along the verge — not on the road or through the fields.'

The khan turned purple with anger, but he couldn't argue with this.

'Aren't there any wise old men in your village? Are they all young idiots like you?'

'Sir,' replied Ashik, bowing respectfully, 'this goat is the oldest creature that we have in the village. You can talk to him, if you like.'

'Well, is there nobody bigger than you then?' shouted the khan.

'This camel,' said Ashik, 'is the tallest by far among us. You may speak with him if you like.'

Karakhan knew that he could not break his word, or he would lose his power as a khan. 'Very well, then, you sharp-wit, I'll let you go. And I'll leave your village alone. But not without some kind of payment. I demand from you a hundred black horses, a hundred robes of the finest brocade and a white yurt with a hundred walls. And I need it all by morning — otherwise you die! Lock him up!' he shouted to his guards.

Ashik was seized at once and locked up, with no hope of calling for help. Or so the khan thought. But Ashik still had the magic pebble that the frog had given him.

'Pebble, pebble,' he whispered, and rubbed the magic green pebble between his fingers, 'let the wicked Karakhan have what he asks — a hundred fine black horses, a hundred brocade robes and a white yurt with a hundred walls.'

To his surprise the pebble crumbled away between his fingers and a beautiful girl appeared in front of him. Her black hair was braided into a long plait and her rosy cheeks dimpled as she smiled.

'Don't worry, Ashik. Karakhan will get all this by morning. But beware! He is an angry, vengeful man. Take these to help you.' She handed him a comb, a needle and a mirror. Then she tossed her long plait over her shoulder and disappeared into thin air.

Before dawn, Karakhan received news that a great caravan had arrived at his palace. They were bringing a hundred brocade robes and all the poles and cloths to set up a white yurt with a hundred walls. They even had all the furniture to go in it! And there were the finest black horses you'd ever seen — a hundred in all, just like the khan had asked for.

When everything was set up ready, the khan himself came out to admire the gifts that had been sent to him. But he was furious that the boy had managed to trick him again.

'You may go,' said the khan coldly to Ashik. But he was determined that the boy should pay for it, and as Ashik set off on foot for home, he soon heard galloping hooves behind him. The khan's guards were riding down upon him, waving their spears. They had set out to kill him!

Ashik felt in his pocket for the gifts that the girl had given him. His hand closed around the comb. He pulled it out and threw it on the ground behind him. Immediately a thick forest sprang up between him and the horsemen. They couldn't find their way through it and had to return to the khan without succeeding in their mission.

'O Mighty Khan! There was a great forest — it was impossible to go any further. Be merciful! We are your loyal servants.'

But Karakhan never showed mercy and he had all the guards executed. A second group was sent out. They found their way around the forest and quickly caught up with Ashik.

'Nothing to it!' said the leader. 'We'll soon have him!'

But at that moment, Ashik pulled out the needle that the girl had given him and threw it down on the ground. A huge mountain rose up between the guards and the boy. Its sides were so steep that they could not climb it and so wide that they could not get around it.

They too were forced to ride back home and tell the khan what had happened. And, once again, the khan wasn't interested in their excuses. He had their heads chopped off.

Now Karakhan decided to tackle the job himself. He would take his wonderful winged horse, called a 'tulpar', which he rode only when the most powerful magic was needed.

The khan mounted the tulpar and away they flew, skimming the forest and the mountains with ease. Soon he spied Ashik ahead of him. Ashik heard the rushing of wings in the sky above him and looked up just in time to see the khan snarling with triumph and brandishing his sword, ready to swoop down and chop off Ashik's head.

Just in time, Ashik managed to throw down the magic mirror, the last of the three gifts that the beautiful girl had given him. At once it spread out into a broad shining lake. The tulpar was caught off balance because he was just coming down to land, and horse and rider fell into the water together.

But Karakhan couldn't swim! Nothing could save him when he tumbled into the water of the lake. The wicked khan drowned right there!

The tulpar, on the other hand, knew exactly how to swim and arrived safely on the shore. He wasn't interested in saving the khan, who had been a cruel master and had often beaten him. No, the tulpar was very pleased to let Ashik climb up on his back and carry him home to his village.

The villagers could hardly believe the news that the khan was dead, but they were full of praise for the young boy who had saved them from ruin.

The aksakals conferred together for a while — it would not be dignified to hurry these things — then finally, nodding their heads sagely, they announced their decision.

'Friends, we have seen how clever this young boy is and how wisely he acted. We are prepared to call him aksakal!'

Everyone clapped and cheered. And from that time on, any person of any age who shows him- or herself wise like Ashik may be called an aksakal.

The Splendours of Samarkand

Everyone on the Silk Road has heard of Samarkand, the city of dreams. And now we're actually entering its gates. Look — there are the famous turquoise domes of the mosques. There is the great market, where silks and spices are traded. And what crowds of people there are in the streets! They come to Samarkand not only to trade but to bring knowledge and news from many lands. You may see learned doctors and astronomers, famous artists, rich merchants and distinguished foreign ambassadors ready to present themselves at the court of the Emperor. For now the greatest emperor of all is ruling — Tamerlane, or Timur, as his subjects call him. Timur means 'iron', and an iron ruler he is, too!

Samarkand has long been a beautiful city. Travellers have always praised its shady gardens, its cool fountains and busy domed markets. Here for centuries traders have displayed their wares from the Silk Road, and Samarkand has always been famous for its own crafts too, especially carpets, glass and fine paper.

Caravans have ridden in and out of here for well over a thousand years. But now the end of the journey is in sight for the Silk Road itself. It is now the beginning of the fifteenth century and this is the last moment of its glory. But in some ways, these are its best days. Today a magnificent caravan of nearly a thousand camels has arrived from China. Chinese traders, Russian merchants and Siberian fur traders have all travelled with it. Already there's great excitement in the town to see what's in the bales that they have brought.

All kinds of marvels are carried along the Silk Road. From Persia and the West come dates, peaches, walnuts, fragrant narcissus flowers, and the mysterious perfumes of frankincense and myrrh. From Central Asia come semi-precious stones such as jade and lapis lazuli. India sends spinach and pepper, sandalwood and an important new material — cotton. China not only sends its silk but trades ginger, millet, roses, camellias, peonies and chrysanthemums.

So — I've carried you on my silken threads all the way from China to Samarkand. But here our journey ends, and I must leave you soon. I have to keep an eye on all those other travellers, stop the demons getting out of control and liven up those sluggish camels in the desert!

They say that the Emperor is giving one of his great feasts tonight. Shall we go? His foreign guests are dining in one of his gorgeous garden palaces. There is wine in plenty, and the guests must drain their golden goblets to the bottom in one gulp. Any guest who can keep it up all evening will be called 'bahadur', or valiant drinker! I wonder if anyone will really be listening to the storytellers tonight?

A Rainbow in Silk

There was once a Beg — an important ruler — who had everything that any man could have wanted. Day and night he was attended by dozens of respectful servants, who bowed low whenever he approached. At his command they hastened to fetch him cooling sherbets to drink or juicy grapes to nibble on. He rode about the city on a magnificent white horse and admired its orchards and gardens, and the fine mosques whose domes gleamed blue and turquoise in the morning sun. His people greeted him warmly wherever he went. At night sumptuous feasts were laid out in decorated pavilions, where charming young girls danced for the Beg and his distinguished guests. The treasuries were full, the harvests were good, the Beg had no foreign enemies to worry about at that time. Whatever he desired, he could have with just one snap of his fingers. But the Beg was very, very bored.

One day he could stand it no longer. He sent for his tried and trusty adviser, a man who had served him well for many years.

'I want something new!' he said, and tears came to his eyes like a spoilt child. 'I'm bored! There's nothing to do any more!'

His counsellor was horrified. 'But, Your Excellency, everything is going so well at present! The people are happy and secure, the fruit is ripening —'

'Yes, yes! That's just it, don't you see? That's why I'm so bored!'

'Well, Your Highness,' said the adviser to the Beg. 'I can order some very fine new conjurors to come to your court tonight to entertain you. I guarantee they will give you pleasure. I myself saw them perform only yesterday and —'

'Oh, I've seen all their tricks!' cried the Beg petulantly, jumping up and stamping his foot.

'Then —' the counsellor was running out of ideas. He had never had to deal with a situation like this before. He scratched his chin anxiously. 'Well,' he said miserably, 'I really don't know, Your Nobleness.'

The Beg looked at him murderously. He could order the old man to be chopped into pieces for saying such a thing! Nobody defied the Beg — nobody! But he knew he was being unfair. Oh, if only there was something new to marvel at!

'Then think of something!' the Beg hissed, and turned away. The counsellor bowed, then retreated thankfully. What had got into his master? But he didn't dare disobey the royal command. Straight away he summoned all the best artists and craftsmen in the town, all the writers and poets, all the tumblers and clowns, all the star-gazers and doctors, and asked their advice.

'Frankly,' he said to them, 'I don't know what to suggest. But please help me to think of something.'

They were all dismayed. It didn't do to have a discontented Beg. Angry Begs in the past had done terrible things, like chopping people's heads off. So they set to work at once.

The star-gazers were the first to come up with a discovery. They were ushered into the Beg's presence.

'We think, Your Highness,' they said, 'that we have found a new star in the sky. We should like to name it after you.'

At first the Beg was excited. 'Show me! Show me tonight!' he said eagerly.

But when he saw it, he was disappointed. 'Oh, it's just like any other star,' he said crossly. 'Call it what you like. But don't call it after me. I am not like any other man.' The Beg had a kind heart but he was a vain man too, and so were many Begs because nobody ever dared to tell them that there was somebody more clever than they were.

Then the tumblers and clowns put on a lavish spectacle: they climbed on top of each other to form human pyramids higher than ever before; they turned more cartwheels and somersaults than ever before; and they cracked jokes that had never been heard in the town before. They had been pestering new arrivals in the city for days, asking all the travellers from distant parts for new jokes. But still the Beg wasn't impressed.

'More of the same!' he said, and got up and left in the middle of the performance, which was really a very rude thing to do.

The doctors gave him potions which they said were recipes for Eternal Life, and which they had mixed with special ingredients to lift the Beg's spirits. But these didn't work.

'Hah! Eternal Life! Well, I shan't know, shall I? Not till you're dead and gone!' And he gave the doctors such a nasty look that they hurried away, afraid that the time might come rather sooner than they expected.

The writers and poets scribbled furiously and begged to be allowed to read their new works to the Beg. But he yawned loudly whenever they tried and even snatched their scrolls away and set light to them, which was a cruel thing to do.

Everybody was losing patience with the Beg, but of course they didn't dare show it. Now their hopes were pinned on the artists and craftsmen.

The glass-blower brought a swan which he had made of fine blue glass, with delicate shading and a pearly finish. Everyone in the court gasped as he carried it in, it was so beautiful. The Beg reached out to snatch it and smash it, but the glass-blower knew about the Beg's temper tantrums by now and managed to keep it just out of his reach.

The carpet weavers worked day and night in teams to complete a fine and huge carpet showing the Beg on his favourite horse. Afterwards people called it the Thirty Day Carpet, for usually it takes months or years to make such a large carpet, and it was a miracle to make one in such a short time. But the Beg wasn't interested and ordered it to be hung up in a far-off pavilion which he rarely visited.

The embroiderers, the jewellers, the tile-makers, the metal-workers all tried to prepare new delights for their lord, but nothing they showed the Beg pleased him.

Finally, he summoned his trusty old adviser again. 'You've got one more day!' he roared at him. 'Don't you understand? I'M BORED! I want something new! By tomorrow! Or else!'

The counsellor was terrified. How could he possibly succeed? He had tried everything he could think of, and everybody with any talent or imagination had worked to please the Beg. How, then, could there be anything new?

The night wore on, and the poor counsellor didn't sleep at all. He tossed and turned and dreamed up crazy schemes, like flying to the moon, or inventing boxes which could be used to talk to people hundreds of miles away — ideas which everyone knew were impossible.

At last the first rays of the morning sun crept through his window. The counsellor's eyes were wet with tears. And as the light touched the teardrops on his eyelashes, suddenly a brilliant rainbow appeared before his eyes.

'That's it!' He sat up in bed, excited beyond belief.

He ran into the Beg's presence and knelt down before him. 'Your Highness, Your Holiness, Your Excellency, I think I can do it! I have had a wonderful idea! Just give me a few more days.'

Even the Beg could see that the counsellor was excited, and he smelt something different in the air. He liked the change of atmosphere. Everyone had been so submissive when they came to see him with their new inventions, as though they, too, were secretly bored with what they could do. Here was this old man who had never invented anything in his life, and plainly he had a new idea. Well, it was worth letting him have a go.

The Beg nodded graciously and dismissed him. That day he enjoyed his breakfast for the first time in months.

The counsellor set teams of silk weavers to work. There was already plenty of silk waiting to be dyed and woven into fine cloth. Little groves of mulberry trees were to be found everywhere in the town and the outlying farmlands, and in season scores of white mulberries plopped down and were squished underfoot as the citizens trod the roads around the town.

He summoned the dyers and told them exactly what to do. Finally the surprise was ready. The counsellor was so pleased and excited that he wasn't even afraid of the Beg now. It had been such fun making his vision a reality!

The counsellor and the chief silk weaver and the Beg's own tailor were ushered into his presence. They didn't let the dyer in, because his hands were always a very strange colour and his clothes always had a rather strong smell, which they thought might upset the Beg.

'Well!' said the Beg eagerly. 'What have you brought me?'

The tailor unrolled, shook out and held up a truly magnificent robe made of the most beautiful, multi-coloured silk. All the colours of the rainbow were in it, all shimmering together, like a real rainbow dancing just in front of your eyes. Even the counsellor gasped with delight. It was even more beautiful than the rainbow he had seen through his teardrops.

Then they all remembered the Beg and looked at him anxiously. They all breathed a huge sigh of relief — a broad smile was slowly spreading over his face. He clapped his hands in delight.

'Yes!' he said triumphantly. 'YES!' he shouted joyfully. 'This is what I've been waiting for! Something really new!' And he put the robe on and twirled around the room in a most un-Beg-like fashion. 'Now I'm not bored any more!'

Then he remembered who he was, and sat down suddenly on his throne and tried to be dignified again. 'Now,' he said, 'I am in a good mood today. So I give permission for everyone in my country to wear clothes made from this rainbow silk whenever they please!' And from that day to this, they have.

*D*ID *Y*OU *K*NOW?

SILK WAS SO PRECIOUS IN CHINA that every year a ceremony was held to worship the goddess of silk, Lei Tsu. The Emperor and Empress rode to her temple with thousands of horsemen carrying silk banners. To show her deep respect for silk-making, the Empress herself looked after a silkworm house, just like the farmers' wives did.

❖ The Romans called their silk robes 'glass togas', but some people were shocked at how light and transparent the material was. Silk dyed purple was the most expensive, and even rich Romans could only afford little strips to sew on to their clothes. Wearing purple silk was only for the most important people in the empire.

❖ From every silk cocoon, a mile of silk thread can be spun. It is important to stop the moth bursting out of the cocoon because that breaks the silk threads, which can then only be used for making 'wild silk', which has a rough finish, or 'floss' silk for padding. That's why the cocoons are dropped into boiling water, to kill the growing pupae. Sometimes people even eat the pupae after they have been 'cooked'!

❖ Silkworms are fussy creatures. Keeping the silkworms happy is an important part of the job. They have to live at exactly the right temperature, and they do not like loud noises or bad smells.

❖ Once the secret of silk had escaped from China, other countries were quick to take it up. The silk of Byzantium became famous, and so did silk from Persia, Damascus, Italy and France. But silk-making is still very important in China today, and you can often buy a silk shirt or dress with a 'Made in China' label inside it.

❖ There are lots of lovely old names for different types of silk cloth. Some of these are samite, sendal, siglaton, baldachin, escariment and boffu. Better-known names are brocade, damask and satin. Some of these names relate to the places where the silk was made, like damask from Damascus and baldachin from Baghdad.

❖ In ancient China, taxes often had to be paid in silk. Sometimes greedy tax officials demanded so much silk that the women in the family could not produce enough. Then the head of the family would be beaten up as a punishment.

❖ Pilgrims who travelled along the Silk Road were often delayed by their hosts along the way, who were eager to hear news from far-off lands. One Buddhist pilgrim, Fa-hsien, set off from China in AD 399 and had to spend several months entertaining a prince who lived on his route. It took Fa-hsien twelve years to reach the Ganges in India.

❖ Water channels along the Silk Road in the western desert areas of what is now China were first carved out over two thousand years ago. Today, in the region of Turpan, there are about a thousand miles of these channels. Pure icy water from snowy mountain springs runs underground into the oasis cities. Here it flows out again into little canals ('karez') that wind around the streets and fields, irrigating crops and fruit trees. They have been in China for a long time, but they were

probably first invented in Persia. The official in charge of the watering system used to be called the Water King.
❖ Silk Road cities in the desert were often abandoned when the water supply ran out, or when they were no longer useful trading posts. They were soon swallowed up by sand, and over the centuries legends grew up about them. Early archaeologists used these tales to guide them to some of the buried cities. In 1895 Sven Hedin, a Swedish scientific explorer, walked for ten days into the Taklamakan Desert in freezing temperatures to find an old city he had heard about. At last he discovered its ruins, still complete with Buddhist wall paintings and statues, and remains of plum and apricot orchards. He was not always so lucky; on another expedition several of his men perished, and he himself nearly died from thirst.
❖ Timur, the great ruler who had his capital at Samarkand, was often known as Tamerlane, or Timur the Lame, because he walked with a limp. He conquered lands in places as far away as Russia, India and Persia. His wives were always richly dressed and beautiful, but he was very jealous of them. Once, so the story goes, he condemned a young architect to death just for kissing the cheek of his bride. And he ordered that women should wear the veil ever after. People in Uzbekistan today still fear the spirit of Timur.
❖ The word 'bandit' comes from the Arabic, meaning 'to cut the road'. Bandits certainly used to 'cut' the Silk Road. The pilgrim Xuanzang arrived at one oasis to find it strewn with the corpses of merchants who had arrived just before him. On another occasion he was able to escape from two hundred Turkish bandits only when they started quarrelling among themselves!
❖ The men who worked with pack animals used their ancient wisdom to keep them alive in the harsh deserts and mountains. They would stock up with herbs and medicines for the horses, to prevent them being upset by the different water that they would have to drink along the way.
❖ Most of the camels on the Eastern and Central Asian stretches of the Silk Road were the two-humped, Bactrian variety. Camels have double lids to their eyes, and nostrils which they can close, which helps to protect them in a sandstorm. They have great powers of endurance. They are bad-tempered animals, though, and camel drivers have to train them thoroughly. A 'rogue' camel is quickly separated from the camel train before it can upset all the others. Arthur Conan Doyle, the writer who invented the detective Sherlock Holmes, wrote about the camel: 'It approaches you with a mildly interested and superior expression... You have just time to say, "The pretty dear is going to kiss me," when two rows of frightful green teeth clash in front of you.'
❖ When ostriches were first imported to China, they were called 'camel-birds'!

SOURCES

THE BRIDE WITH THE HORSE'S HEAD

Chinese Gods — Keith Stevens, Collins and Brown 1997
New Larousse Encyclopaedia of Mythology — Paul Hamlyn 1959

MONKEY AND THE RIVER DRAGON

Monkey — Wu Ch'eng-en, translated by Arthur Waley, Penguin 1942
Journey to the West — translated by Anthony C. Yu, University of Chicago Press 1977
Xuan Zang: A Buddhist Pilgrim on the Silk Road — Sally Hovey Wriggins, West View Press 1996

WHITE CLOUD FAIRY

Tales from Dunhuang — compiled by Chen Yu, New World Press, Beijing 1989
Dunhuang — Roderick Whitfield, Textile and Art Publications 1995

THE ENCHANTED GARDEN

Mirror of the Invisible World: Tales from the Khamseh of Nizami — Peter J. Chelkowski, New York Metropolitan Museum of Art 1975

THE MAGIC SADDLEBAG

Folk Tales of Central Asia — Amina Shah, Octagon Press 1970
Caravans to Tartary — Roland and Sabrina Michaud, Thames and Hudson 1978

CLEVER ASHIK

Folk Tales from the Soviet Union: Central Asia and Kazakhstan — Raduga Publishers, Moscow 1986
Kyrgyzstan — series editor Mary M. Rodgers, Tom Streissguth and Colleen Sexton, Lerner Publications Co.

A RAINBOW IN SILK

Oral tradition, Uzbekistan. Expanded from version told by local guide.

GENERAL

Central Asia: A Traveller's Companion — Kathleen Hopkirk, John Murray 1993
Foreign Devils on the Silk Road — Peter Hopkirk, Oxford University Press 1980
The Silk Road — Louis Boulnois, George Allen and Unwin Ltd 1966
The Silk Road: A History — Irene M. Franck and David M. Brownstone, Facts on File Publications 1986
The Silk Road: Illustrated Guide — Judy Bonavia, Collins 1988